TITANICAT

Marty Crisp · Illustrated by Robert Papp

SLEEPING BEAR PRESS

TITANIC WAS A SHIP AS BIG AS HER NAME. SHE WAS TEN STORIES HIGH AND FOUR BLOCKS LONG, A FLOATING CITY WITH HER OWN RESTAURANT, POST OFFICE, LIBRARY, SWIMMING POOL, SQUASH COURTS, GYMNASIUM, AND EVEN A TURKISH BATH. THE NEW SHIP CARRIED SOME OF THE WORLD'S RICHEST PEOPLE, AS WELL AS POOR IMMIGRANTS FROM IRELAND, SWEDEN, NORWAY, CROATIA, BULGARIA, PORTUGAL, AND SYRIA AMONG ITS 2,228 PASSENGERS AND CREW. BECAUSE SHE WAS BUILT WITH WATERTIGHT COMPARTMENTS IN HER HULL, PEOPLE THOUGHT *TITANIC* WAS "UNSINKABLE."

BUT THE HUGE OCEAN LINER HIT AN ICEBERG AS SHE STEAMED ACROSS THE NORTH ATLANTIC ON HER MAIDEN VOYAGE. IT WAS A

MOONLESS NIGHT—APRIL 15, 1912—WHEN THE SHIP SANK, TAKING WITH HER SOME 1,500 PEOPLE, A FORTUNE IN CARGO, AT LEAST NINE DOGS, AND, JUST POSSIBLY, A CAT.

AS FAR AS HISTORY WAS CONCERNED, *TITANIC*'S CAT—BECAUSE EVERY SHIP THAT SAILED IN THOSE DAYS HAD A CAT ON BOARD— COULD BE COUNTED AMONG THE DEAD. FOR 80 YEARS THE TRUE FATE OF THE CAT WAS JUST ANOTHER OF *TITANIC*'S UNSOLVED MYS- TERIES, RESTING WITH THE RUSTING HULK ON THE OCEAN FLOOR.

THEN IN 1985, EXPLORER ROBERT BALLARD DISCOVERED THE LONG-LOST WRECK AND NEW INFORMATION BEGAN SURFACING. LIKE THIS STORY. . . .

Every time Jim glanced to the side, there was the cat, flashing the tip of her tortoiseshell tail at him, all the way to the shipyard. Some claimed a tortoiseshell cat could see the future. Jim, himself, believed only that cats were lucky. His Da worked in the Belfast shipyard, so Jim knew all the lore about ships and their cats.

Jim reached the ship, rocking in its slip, towering above him. Its fresh black-and-white paint seemed to glow in the morning sun. Jim felt lucky to be crewing this beauty on her first voyage. It was his first voyage, too.

Jim's eyes started with the four tall smokestacks, studying every detail as his gaze slowly traveled down to the dock. The same cat was sitting there on top of a piling. She jumped down and came towards Jim as if she'd been waiting for him all along. It was a good omen for a cat to walk towards you. Jim was certain this was going to be a great trip.

He held out his hand. His Da said Jim had a way with animals. The cat rubbed against his knees as he tickled her soft fur.

Then the cat turned and disappeared into the open hatch on the side of the ship. A man in a blue uniform came up behind Jim. "Did you see our cat?"

"Aye, I did, sir." Jim nodded at the ship. "She just went inside."

"Are you here to crew for the trials, lad?"

"I'm signed on as cabin boy, sir. Name's Jim Mulholland. I'll be going all the way to America!" Jim couldn't keep the excitement out of his voice.

"Welcome aboard." The man smiled and shook Jim's hand. "I'm Chief Steward Latimer, and from this moment on, you're in charge of that fool cat."

"Aye, aye, sir. I'll find old 4-0-1 as soon as I stow my gear." It was a long-standing superstition not to call a ship by name while it was being built. That could be unlucky. Every ship under construction had a number. This ship was 4-0-1, and the cat would be called likewise.

There were a lot of places to look for a cat on a ship four city blocks long. Jim searched from the compass platform on the boat deck to the boiler rooms at the bottom of the ship. The smell of fresh varnish was strong in the third class general room. But no cat.

Jim's whistle echoed back to him under the glass dome of the Grand Staircase. But no cat.

Jim sighed with relief when he finally found the tortoiseshell on B-deck in Café Parisian. Then he saw a kitten beside her.

"So you have family! It's a fine job you've done, little 4-0-1."

Jim knelt and stroked each fluffy kitten: four new ship's cats in all. This voyage would be lucky indeed.

Jim kept the little cat family in a box the next day as he polished chairs on A-deck. The sharp tang of sea air made him daydream about the great voyage to come. He had always wanted to go to sea and see faraway places. First there would be two weeks of fitting out and sprucing up, then the launch and the ship's trials would begin.

Jim worked hard, keeping the cat family close at hand.

Once the ship got moving, he noticed that 4-0-1 would

slip in and out of the box, putting an end to mice scurrying

through the galleys. She caught a rat in an oatmeal bin Jim

had forgotten to cover in the third-class storage cupboard.

It was lucky she was around, he suspected, to keep him

from getting into trouble.

Jim filled the water tanks above the porcelain sinks in each third-class stateroom. "Oh, Danny boy, the pipes, the pipes are calling," he sang as he worked. The kittens frisked to the lilt of the Irish lullaby, and the cat seemed to study Jim as he sang.

Jim was on the boat deck, swabbing it clean with a mop,

when he spotted one tiny bold kitten venturing out of the

box and ducking under a lifeboat. There was no railing

where the lifeboats hung. What if the kitten fell overboard?

Jim squatted by the lifeboat and used his mop to pull the kitten back to safety. 4-0-1 watched it all with her mysterious green eyes. She began licking her baby clean as soon as Jim put it in the box, as if nothing had happened at all. But Jim always heard the rumble of her purr now whenever he came close.

So he was surprised when he stood at the rail, two days later, watching the ship dock in Southampton. The cat was not at her usual spot beside him. Her kittens were sleeping down below, in the box under his bunk, as they'd done during the eight days of practicing stops and turns and night running.

"Have you seen 4-0-1?" Jim asked the porters and the deckhands. No one had, and passengers were starting to come aboard.

"Have you seen 4-0-1?" he asked Mr. Latimer. But the Chief Steward only shook his head, too busy to answer.

Jim leaned forward in surprise. Could that be his cat,

going down the gangplank, carrying a kitten in her mouth?

Jim shaded his eyes. It was her! She placed her kitten in a

coil of rope on the dock and streaked back into the ship.

He could hear her loud mewing, even from here. A mewing

cat meant a difficult journey. Jim knew the old sailors'

superstition as well as he knew his Da's Irish lullabies.

He clutched the rail as she reappeared with a second kitten.

First-class women in silks and furs and third-class men in rough brown wool streamed onto the ship. Jim pushed through the crowd, hurrying down to his berth. Even here, far below deck, he could smell saltwater and fish. It was getting close to cast-off time, but the ship couldn't start her maiden voyage without her ship's cat.

Jim found only one kitten. It was the one he'd rescued from under the lifeboat. He picked it up and cradled it. Surely 4-0-1 would come back. As he stroked the kitten's fur, he could hear people calling, "*Bon voyage!* Send me a postcard!"

The call of "all ashore who's going ashore" startled Jim.

He looked down at the kitten cupped in his hands.

There was really no other choice. Jim bounded up the

stairs and raced across the deck.

"You're gonna' miss the boat, boy," a crewman called.

The gangplank was already being hauled in. Jim clutched

the kitten and jumped.

An ear-splitting blast from the ship's whistle told Jim the ship was on its way. It was sailing with his duffel bag and all his gear still on board. He wouldn't be crossing the Atlantic after all. He wouldn't be seeing America.

"I think you forgot someone," Jim muttered, glowering down at 4-0-1. "I hope you're happy. Now look what you've made me do."

The cat looked up at him, unblinking.

"Well, the *Titanic* is one ship that doesn't need a fool ship's cat for luck. She's unsinkable. The finest ship ever built."

The cat didn't glance up as tugboats pulled the *Titanic* into Southampton harbor. She was busy licking her kittens.

Six days later Jim was hard at work delivering packages so he could rent a room for himself and the little cat family. The cat was his friend, despite what she'd done. He'd taken care of 4-0-1 and her kittens on board *Titanic*, and he'd keep taking care of them until they could find another ship—a smaller, older, less-exciting ship to be sure.

Jim was so busy delivering bread and milk, newspapers and dry goods parcels, that he missed the first whispers of trouble.

But the whispers soon turned into cries. Jim waited with the crowd in Canute Street, outside the White Star offices. Grim men in suits came out and said the *Titanic* had hit an iceberg. They posted the survivors' names.

The kittens slept in a warm lump in the canvas bag Jim had slung over his shoulder. The cat followed close on his heels as he threaded his way through the throng to get a closer look at the lists tacked to the door of the White Star Line. One sheet said "Saved." It was the shortest. The other said "Missing." Jim's eyes scanned the long columns. His name was there.

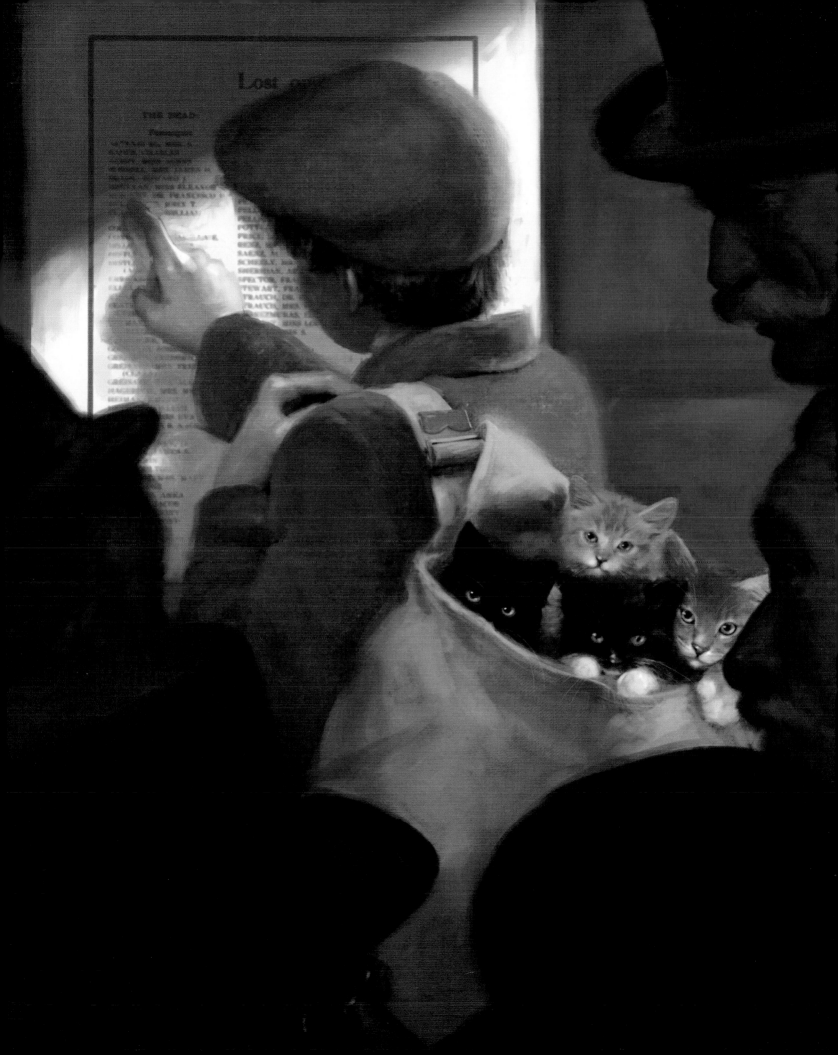

Jim scooped up the cat and looked into her bottomless green eyes. "You gave me your luck," Jim whispered. "And I thank you." The cat blinked and went back to licking her whiskers.

There was really nothing else to say.

To Ainslee Rose Crisp, born February 5, 2008

—M. C.

For everyone who remembers to listen to their own furry friend

—R. P.

AUTHOR'S NOTE

With the 1997 publication of the memoir of *Titanic* stewardess Violet Jessop, historians learned that a ship's cat had given birth to a litter of four kittens before the *Titanic* was launched, and was on board with those kittens in the early spring of 1912.

This report was followed by an article in the Belfast Irish News by reporter Anne Hailes. She interviewed 92-year-old Paddy Scott, who had, himself, once been a reporter. In the 1930s, Scott said, he'd talked with an Irishman who claimed he'd crewed *Titanic*'s trials and was assigned the care of the ship's cat. When the cat got off in Southampton, taking her kittens with her, the superstitious young sailor followed.

For details about the *Titanic*, my primary sources included experts George Behe (*Safety, Speed and Sacrifice*), and Walter Lord (*A Night to Remember* and *The Night Lives On*). I was lucky to meet and talk with *Titanic* survivor Elizabeth Gladys "Millvina" Dean and explorer Robert Ballard (*The Disaster of the Titanic*) at the 35th anniversary of the *Titanic* Historical Society. I visited the Society's museum in Indian Orchard, Massachusetts; the maritime museum in Southampton, England; the maritime museum in Los Angeles, California, with its detailed cutaway model of the ship; and special *Titanic* exhibitions in Orlando, Florida; Atlantic City, New Jersey; Newport News, Virginia; and on the *Queen Mary*, in Long Beach, California.

Written primary source material came from survivor accounts:

Gracie, Colonel Archibald, Titanic, *A Survivor's Story*, 1998, Academy Chicago Publishers, Chicago, Ill. (first published as *The Truth About the Titanic* in 1913).

Jessop, Violet, *Titanic Survivor*, 1997, Sheridan House, Dobbs Ferry, N.Y.

O'Donnell, D. D., *The Last Days of the Titanic*, 1997, Wolfhound Press, Dublin, Ireland (O'Donnell was aboard, but got off before the ocean crossing).

Thayer, John B., *The Sinking of the S.S. Titanic*, 1998, Academy Chicago Publishers, Chicago, Ill. (first published in 1940).

Winocour, Jack, editor, *The Story of the Titanic As Told by Its Survivors*, 1960, Dover Publications, NYC.

Text Copyright © 2008 Marty Crisp
Illustration Copyright © 2008 Robert Papp

All rights reserved. No part of this book may be reproduced in any manner without the express written consent of the publisher, except in the case of brief excerpts in critical reviews and articles. All inquiries should be addressed to:

Sleeping Bear Press™

310 North Main Street, Suite 300
Chelsea, MI 48118
www.sleepingbearpress.com

© 2008 Sleeping Bear Press is an imprint of Gale, a part of Cengage Learning.

Printed and bound in China.

10 9 8 7 6 5 4 3 2 1

ISBN: 978-1-58536-355-1
Library of Congress Cataloging-in-Publication Data

Crisp, Marty.
Titanicat / written by Marty Crisp ; illustrated by Robert Papp. --
1st ed.
p. cm.
Summary: A boy who has signed on as cabin boy aboard the *Titanic* helps ready the ship for its maiden voyage, but when it is time to set sail and he cannot find the ship's cat on board, he leaves to search for her.
ISBN 978-1-58536-355-1
[1. Cats--Fiction. 2. Titanic (Steamship)--Fiction.] I. Papp, Robert, ill. II. Title.

PZ7.C86942Ti 2008
[E]--dc22
2007047622.